THIS WALKER BOOK BELONGS TO:

# For Jennie Fojtik

First published 2005 by Walker Books Ltd, 87 Vauxhall Walk, London SE11 5HJ

This edition published 2006

4 6 8 10 9 7 5 3

Text © 2005 Joyce Dunbar
Illustrations © 2005 Polly Dunbar

The right of Joyce Dunbar and Polly Dunbar to be identified as author and illustrator respectively
of this work has been asserted by them in accordance with the Copyright, Designs and Patents Act 1988

This book has been typeset in Godlike Emboldened

Printed in China

British Library Cataloguing in Publication Data: a catalogue record for
this book is available from the British Library

ISBN 978-1-4063-0161-8

www.walkerbooks.co.uk

www.joycedunbar.com   www.pollydunbar.com

WALKER BOOKS
AND SUBSIDIARIES
LONDON · BOSTON · SYDNEY · AUCKLAND

# Shoe Baby

## Joyce Dunbar

illustrated by
## Polly Dunbar

There once was a baby
Who hid in a shoe
And had learnt how to say,
"How do you do?"

In a shoe you might think
There is not much to do,
But this very same baby
Went to SEA in that shoe!

A dolphin came by
And an octopus too.
Said this sail-away baby,
"How do you do?"

And this baby I tell you
Went to TOWN in that shoe,
Passing the shops
On the way to the zoo.

At the monkeys he waved
And the elephants too
And he greeted them all
With a "How do you do?"

This very same baby
FLEW in that shoe!
To the birds of the air he said,
"How do you do?"

Then this fly-away baby
SANG in the shoe.
"Dum-de-dum. Tra-la-la.
How do you do?"

Later, this baby
Had TEA in that shoe!
He invited the Queen
Who brought the King too.

"Good gracious!" they said,
"Pray who are you?"
With a bow said the baby,
"How do you do?"

At long last this baby
Slept in that shoe
So dozy, so cosy,
So tickety-boo.

And he dreamed a bright dream
Of a pink cockatoo
Saying over and over,
"Toodle-oo! Toodle-oo!"

But now ... there's a noise ...
"BOO-HOO-HOO!
BOO-HOO-HOO!"
And a giant comes by
Wearing only one shoe.

And he makes such a fuss
Such a hullabaloo,
Stamping and shouting,
"WHO TOOK
MY SHOE?"

And following fast
Came a giantess too,
Sobbing and sighing,
"BOO-HOO-HOO!
BOO-HOO-HOO!"

And into her polka-dot
Hankie she blew,
"My baby! He's lost!
Oh what shall I do?"

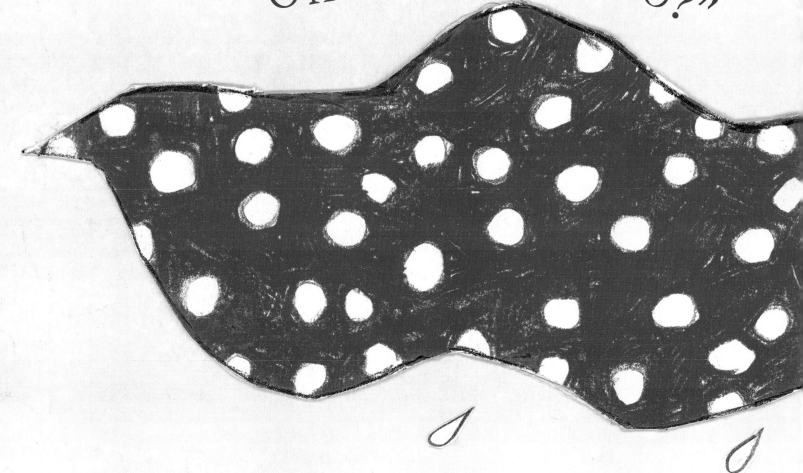

All at once this strange baby

Grew in the shoe.

He grew
and he grew

# Right out of that shoe!

"Peekaboo!" said the baby,
Popping up from the shoe.
"Hey Papa!
Hey Mama!
How do
you
do?"

"My shoe," said Papa.
"My runaway shoe!
I could find only one,
But now I have two!"

"My baby," said Mama.
"It really is you!
High and low I have looked
but not in a shoe!"

And the baby
just beamed
and said,

"How do you do?"

WALKER BOOKS is the world's leading
independent publisher of children's books.
Working with the best authors and illustrators
we create books for all ages, from babies
to teenagers – books your child will
grow up with and always remember. So…

FOR THE BEST CHILDREN'S BOOKS,
LOOK FOR THE BEAR